The Little Nut Tree

Sally Gardner

Orion
Children's Books

To Lydia, Freya and Dominic, with love

Published in paperback in 1999
First published in Great Britain in 1993
by Orion Children's Books
A division of the Orion Publishing Group Ltd
Orion House
5 Upper St Martin's Lane
London WC2H 9EA

A catalogue for this book is available from the British Library

Printed and bound in India

For my birthday I was sent a little tree

I dug a hole

I planted it

I watered it

I tended it with care

Summer came and went

Autumn too

Winter followed

Then spring

Then one morning I looked out of the window

There was my tree in all its glory

Papa thought we should talk to his friend Mr Albert

When we told him, Mr Albert came to look for himself

He asked if he might bring some gentlemen to see it

They came straight away

The news of my little nut tree spread far and wide

Everyone was talking

about my tree

Soon a crowd had gathered

all for the sake of my little nut tree

Then one day a special letter arrived . . .

The princess walked into our house

and went straight to the nut tree

She wanted to take it home with her

The grand people told me

I could give no greater gift

so I gave my little nut tree to the King of Spain's daughter

Two footmen dug up my nut tree and carried it away

I felt very sad

Then I saw the golden twig

I flew on golden wings

I skipped over water

I danced over sea

All the birds in the air couldn't catch me

When I got home

I put my golden twig in a pot

and went upstairs

to bed

In the morning

you wouldn't believe what I saw!

Another little nut tree – just for me!

I had a little nut tree
Nothing would it bear
But a silver nutmeg
And a golden pear

The King of Spain's daughter
Came to visit me
All for the sake
Of my little nut tree

I skipped over water
I danced over sea
All the birds in the air
Couldn't catch me